For my daughter, Dr. Cissy Burnside,
a veterinarian who's the cat's meow
—P.M.

To beautiful Madison
—R.C.

2505036

THIS IS A BORZOI BOOK PUBLISHED BY ALFRED A. KNOPF

Text copyright © 2005 by Pat Mora
Illustrations copyright © 2005 by Raul Colón
All rights reserved under International and Pan-American Copyright Conventions. Published in the
United States by Alfred A. Knopf, an imprint of Random House Children's Books, a division of
Random House, Inc., New York, and simultaneously in Canada by Random House of Canada
Limited, Toronto. Distributed by Random House, Inc., New York.
www.randomhouse.com/kids
KNOPF, BORZOI BOOKS, and the colophon are registered trademarks of Random House, Inc.

Library of Congress Cataloging-in-Publication Data
Mora, Pat.
Doña Flor : a tall tale about a giant woman with a great big heart /
by Pat Mora ; illustrated by Raul Colón.
p. cm.
SUMMARY: Doña Flor, a giant lady with a big heart, sets off to protect her neighbors from what
they think is a dangerous animal, but soon discovers the tiny secret behind the huge noise.
[1. Giants—Fiction. 2. Puma—Fiction. 3. Villages—Fiction. 4. Tall tales.] I. Colón, Raul, ill. II. Title.
PZ7.M78819Don 2005
[E]—dc22
2005040794

ISBN 0-375-82337-9 (trade)
ISBN 0-375-92337-3 (lib. bdg.)
ISBN 0-679-98002-4 (Span. lib. bdg.)
ISBN 0-440-41768-6 (Span. pbk.)

MANUFACTURED IN CHINA
October 2005
10 9 8 7 6 5 4 3 2 1
First Edition

A TALL TALE ABOUT A GIANT WOMAN WITH A GREAT BIG HEART

DOÑA FLOR

by **Pat Mora** · illustrated by **Raul Colón**

Alfred A. Knopf · New York

Every winter morning when the sun opened one eye, Doña Flor grabbed a handful of snow from the top of a nearby mountain. *"Brrrrrrrrr,"* she said, rubbing the snow on her face to wake up.

Long, long ago, when Flor was a baby, her mother sang to her in a voice sweet as river music. When Flor's mother sang to her corn plants, they grew tall as trees, and when she sang to her baby, her sweet flower, well, Flor grew and grew, too.

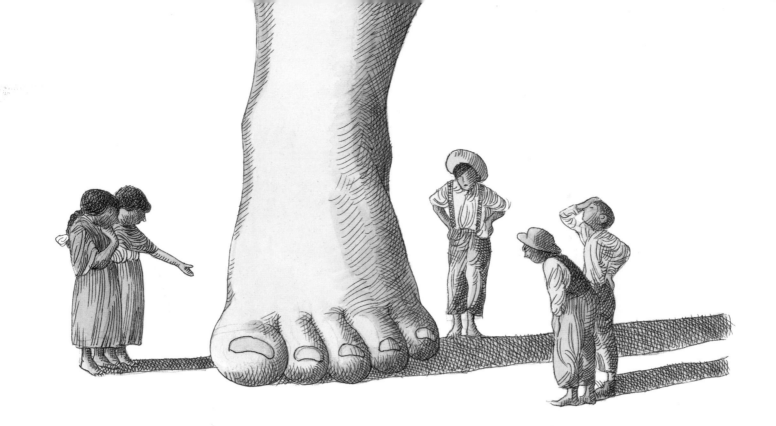

Some children laughed at her because she was different. "*¡Mira!* Look! Big Foot!" they called when she walked by.

"Flor talks funny," they whispered, because Flor spoke to butterflies and grasshoppers. She spoke every language, even rattler.

But soon Flor's friends and neighbors asked her for help. Children late for school asked, "*Por favor,* Flor, could you give us a ride?" She took just one of her giant steps and was at the school door. Of course, the *escuela* shook and the windows rattled.

When Flor finally stopped growing, she built her own
house, *una casa* big as a mountain and open as a canyon.
She scooped a handful of dirt and made herself a valley for
mixing clay, straw, and water. She added some *estrellas*. The
stars made the adobe shine. When she worked, Flor sang,
and birds came and built nests in her hair. Flor wanted
everyone to feel at home in her house. *"Mi casa es su casa,"*
she said to people, animals, and plants, so they knew they
were always welcome. Everyone called her *Doña* Flor
because they respected her.

No one needed an alarm clock in Doña Flor's *pueblo.*
When her hands, wide as plates, started pat-pat-patting
tortillas, everyone in the village woke up. So her neighbors
would have plenty to eat, she stacked her tortillas on the
huge rock table in front of her house.

Flor's tortillas were the biggest, bestest tortillas in the
whole wide world. People used the extra ones as roofs.
Mmmm, the houses smelled corn-good when the sun was
hot. In the summer, the children floated around the pond on
tortilla rafts.

One warm spring day, while a family of lizards swept her house, Doña Flor brought out her stacks of fresh tortillas. Nobody came. *Hmmmmmmm,* thought Flor. She started knocking on doors and calling to her neighbors.

"*¿Qué pasa?* What's the matter?" she asked, bending down to peer into their small doors to see where they were hiding.

"*¡El puma!*" they whispered. "The children have heard a huge mountain lion circling the village. Listen!"

Flor listened, and sure enough, she heard a terrible "*Rrrr-oarrr!*"

Doña Flor and her animal friends went out looking for the huge *gato,* but they couldn't find it. That night, she carried her tired friends, the coyotes and rabbits, back home. But just as she started to tuck them in and read them a good-night story, they all heard, *"Rrrr-oarrr!"*

"Where *is* that darn cat?" asked Flor, but the scared animals were shaking and shivering under their sheets. She gave each a giant kiss.

SMACK! The sound echoed and woke the grumpy wind, who stormed up and down the hills a-grumblin' and a-growlin'. That night, the wind got so angry that he blew the trees and houses first to the left and then to the right, again to the left and then to the right.

Now, Doña Flor liked her sleep, so she wasn't smiling when she heard the wind spinnin' round and around the village. Together, the wind and the giant cat roared all night, and nobody got much sleep.

As the sun rose, Flor's neighbors, shaking at the commotion, peered out their windows. Tired-looking Flor was giving that wind a big hug to quiet him down. Then she started her morning chores.

Doña Flor had work to do. But first she looked around the village. Where were her neighbors? Then she heard, *"Rrrr-oarrr! Rrrr-oarrr!"*

Flor stomped off to find the puma that was bothering her *amigos.*

Exhausted by afternoon, Doña Flor still hadn't found that cat, so she sat outside the library for a rest. She was too big to fit inside, so she just reached in the window for books. You see, Flor was probably the fastest reader ever. Why, she could read the whole encyclopedia in five minutes. She liked to sit in the shade and read stories and poems nice and slow to the children and animals that climbed all over her soft body. Today, she called and called, and finally the children came, but they were scared.

What can I do to cheer my friends up? wondered Flor as she saw their frightened faces. She thought and thought. Now, Flor knew that her village needed *un río,* a river, so to make her neighbors happy, Doña Flor scratched a new riverbed with her thumb. When the water trickled down the stones for the first time, Flor called out, "Just listen to that! Isn't that the prettiest sound you've ever heard?" She smiled, and her smile was about as big as her tortillas, but today her neighbors could barely smile back. They were too worried about the mountain lion, and sure enough, suddenly there was a terrible *"Rrrr-oarrr! Rrrr-oarrr!"*

That's it! thought Doña Flor, and again she stomped off to look for the giant puma, but she still couldn't find him. She went home to think and work in her garden. It was like a small forest on the edge of the *pueblo,* a tangle of poppies, morning glories, roses, luscious tomatoes, and *chiles.* Whatever she planted grew so fast, you could hear the roots spreading at night. Her neighbors used the sunflowers as bright yellow umbrellas. She gave the school band her hollyhocks to use as trumpets. The music smelled like spring.

"My plants grow that big because I sing to them like my mother did," Doña Flor told the children when they came three at a time to carry home an ear of corn. But today, the children ran home when they heard, *"Rrrr-oarrr!"* The sound rattled all the plates in the *pueblo.* Flor's neighbors' teeth started rattling, too.

Where is that big monster gato? Doña Flor wondered. The smell of roses helped Flor think, so she went inside and took a long, hot bubble bath. Everyone knew Doña Flor was thinking when bubbles that smelled like roses began to rise from her chimney.

I know, thought Flor, *I'll go to my animal friends for help.* She stomped off again, and she started asking because, remember, she spoke every language, even rattler.

"Go quietly to the tallest mesa," said the deer.

"Vaya silencios-s-s-amente a la mes-s-s-a mas-s-s alta," hissed the snake.

"Go quietly to the tallest mesa," whispered the rabbits.

Knowing that animals are mighty smart, Doña Flor
followed their advice. She walked very, very softly up to
the tallest mesa. She looked around carefully for the giant
cat. Then right near her she heard, *"Rrrr-oarrr! Rrrr-oarrr!"*
Flor jumped so high, she bumped into the sun and gave him
a black eye.

Flor looked around. All she saw was the back of a cute little puma. She watched him very quietly. Doña Flor began to tiptoe toward the puma when all of a sudden he roared into a long, hollow log. The sound became a huge *"Rrrr-oarrr!"* that echoed down into the valley.

Now, the little puma thought the loud noise was so funny that he rolled on his back and started laughing and laughing—until he saw big Doña Flor.

Aha! thought Flor. "Are you the *chico* who's causing all the trouble?" she asked. The little puma tried to look very fierce. His eyes sizzled with angry sparks. He opened his mouth wide, and his teeth glinted. He roared his meanest roar. *"Rrrr-oarrr!"* he growled, but without the log, the growl wasn't really very fierce.

Doña Flor just smiled at that brave cat and said, "Why, you're just a kitten to me, Pumito," and she bent down and scratched that puma behind the ears, and she whispered to him in cat talk until that cat began to purr and *purrrrrrrrr.* Pumito began to lick Flor's face with his wet tongue.

Suddenly Flor heard a new noise. "*Doña Flor, ¿dónde estás?* Where are you?" called her worried neighbors. Even though they were frightened, they had all come, holding hands, looking for her.

"Meet my new *amigo,*" said Doña Flor, smiling at her thoughtful neighbors.

That evening, Flor plucked a star the way she always did and plunked it on the tallest tree so her friends in the *pueblo* could find their way home. She plucked *una estrella* to put above her door, too. Even the stars could hear Doña Flor humming.

Flor liked a fresh bed, so she reached up and filled her arms with clouds smelling of flowery breezes. She shaped the clouds into a soft, deep bed and into hills of puffy pillows. *"Mmmm,"* said Flor as she snuggled in the clouds.

"Tonight, I'm very tired after my adventure with the giant cat, right, Pumito?" chuckled Doña Flor. All the animals snuggled down with her, and Pumito stretched out over her big toes.

PAT MORA, who writes poetry, nonfiction, and children's books, is the author of *Tomás and the Library Lady,* also illustrated by Raul Colón, and *A Library for Juana,* illustrated by Beatriz Vidal. A recipient of a National Endowment for the Arts Poetry Fellowship and a Kellogg National Fellowship, Ms. Mora is a native of El Paso, Texas, and currently lives in Santa Fe, where, in addition to her full-time writing, she also works as an advocate for multicultural education. Ms. Mora speaks about literature and literacy to teachers, librarians, and children of all ages around the country. You can find out more about her at www.patmora.com.

RAUL COLÓN has illustrated many wonderful picture books for children, and his style is one that has become highly recognized and sought-after both in book publishing and in commercial advertising. Working with an intriguing combination of watercolor washes, etching, and colored and litho pencils, Mr. Colón has once again created beautiful illustrations that will captivate and entertain both children and adults. This is his second collaboration with Pat Mora; their first, *Tomás and the Library Lady,* received the Tomás Rivera Mexican-American Children's Book Award. Mr. Colón lives in New City, New York.